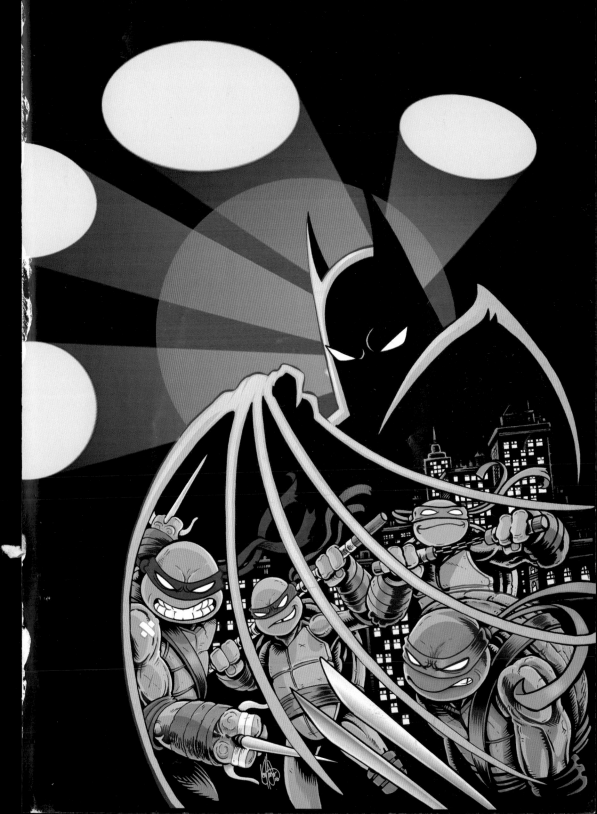

Raintree is an imprint of Capstone Global Library
Limited, a company incorporated in England and
Wales having its registered office at 264 Banbury
Road, Oxford, OX2 7DY – Registered company number:
6695582

www.raintree.co.uk
myorders@raintree.co.uk

Originally published as BATMAN/TEENAGE MUTANT NINJA
TURTLES ADVENTURES issue #3.

Edited by Donald Lemke and Gena Chester
Designed by Hilary Wacholz
Production by Kathy McColley
Originated by Capstone Global Library Ltd
Printed and bound in India

ISBN 978 1 4747 6649 4
22 21 20 19 18
10 9 8 7 6 5 4 3 2 1

British Library Cataloguing in Publication Data
A full catalogue record for this book is available from
the British Library.

Batman created by Bob Kane with Bill Finger

BATMAN TEENAGE MUTANT NINJA TURTLES ADVENTURES

GREENER ON THE OTHER SIDE

WRITER: **MATTHEW K. MANNING** | ARTIST: **JON SOMMARIVA**
INKER: **SEAN PARSONS** | COLOURIST: **LEONARDO ITO**

raintree
a Capstone company — publishers for children

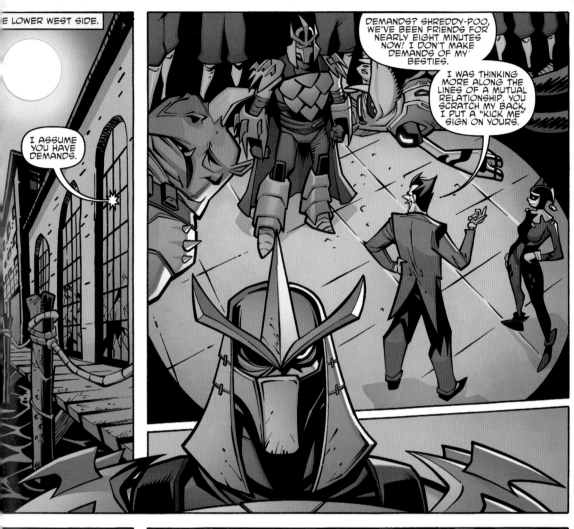

LOWER WEST SIDE.

I ASSUME YOU HAVE DEMANDS.

DEMANDS? SHREDDY-POO, WE'VE BEEN FRIENDS FOR NEARLY EIGHT MINUTES NOW! I DON'T MAKE DEMANDS OF MY BESTIES.

I WAS THINKING MORE ALONG THE LINES OF A MUTUAL RELATIONSHIP. YOU SCRATCH MY BACK, I PUT A "KICK ME" SIGN ON YOURS.

TALL, DARK, AND SILENT, HUH? YOU KNOW, YOU'RE JUST MY TYPE.

BUT LET'S BE HONEST NOW, SWISS ARMY HELMET, THIS TOWN OF YOURS, WELL, IT'S MY TYPE, TOO.

JUST THE EASE OF FINDING EXPLOSIVES ALONE. WHY, IT'S A BREATH OF FRESH AIR!

Panel 1: YOU KNOW WHAT? YOU'VE SOLD ME! I'LL TAKE THE WHOLE SHEBANG! WRAP IT UP, WILL YOU?

Panel 2: I WANT NOTHING TO DO WITH—

YOU'VE ALREADY MADE THE DEAL, MAN. DON'T OVERSELL IT!

Panel 3:

TIGER CLAW.

RAHZAR.

FISHFACE.

BAXTER STOCKMAN.

Mutants. Shredder loyalists. Potentially the world's creepiest bobsled team.

Panel 4: OH. I SEE YOU'VE BROUGHT ALONG THE WHOLE DYSFUNCTIONAL FAMILY.

LOOK! THAT ONE'S A KITTY! CAN I PET THE KITTY, PUDDIN'?

Panel 5: ONLY IF YOU DON'T VALUE YOUR HAND, YOU—

YOU KNOW, MAYBE THIS MEETING OF THE UNSTABLE MINDS WASN'T THE KEENEST IDEA.

TELL YOU WHAT, YOU GRANT MY GAL FRIDAY AND ME SAFE PASSAGE, AND I WON'T BRING THIS WHOLE PLACE CRASHING DOWN ON YOUR LITTLE ZOO CREW.

8

WHAT SAY? *SPIT SHAKE?*

NO? THEN HOW 'BOUT A KISS FOR OLD AUNT PETUNIA?

HUH. HUH HU... HA.

NOW DON'T YOU START. IF YOU START LAUGHING, YOU'LL GET ME GOING.

BUT SERIOUSLY, FOLKS... LET'S SEE WHO WE HAVE IN THE AUDIENCE TODAY.

YOU! YOU SEEM LIKE YOU'VE GOT A GOOD OVERSIZED HEAD ON YOUR SHOULDERS. LET ME ASK YOU A QUESTION.

HOW DO I GET ME A PAIR OF THOSE?

BATWOMAN IS RIGHT. BATGIRL.

SO IS IT MISS BATGIRL, OR MRS. BATGIRL OR BATGIRL WITH A SERIOUS BOYFRIEND WHO ISN'T LOOKING FOR—?

DONNIE.

WHUMP

BATGIRL IS RIGHT. SNAKEWEED'S NEVER BEEN THE BRIGHTEST BULB IN THE FLOWER GARDEN.

NOW HE'S BIGGER, AND FIGHTING WITH A PRECISION WE'VE NOT SEEN BEFORE.

BECAUSE HE'S NOT IN THE DRIVER'S SEAT.

WE'LL KEEP SNAKEWEED BUSY.

pfft

ROBIN...

..., YOU TAKE THE FIGHT TO IVY.

WHOA. WHO DISHED OUT THE WEED KILLER?

THAT WOULD BE US.

≈COUGH≈ ≈COUGH≈

HE'S NOT BEING LITERAL.

≈COUGH≈

OKAY, ONCE SHE'S THROUGH THE PORTAL, WE SHOULD HAVE A GOOD TEN MINUTES BEFORE IT DISAPPEARS.

FWASH

UM...?

OKAY, SCRATCH THAT. MAKE THAT TEN SECONDS. TEN SECONDS UNTIL IT DISAPPEARS.

SORRY, EVERYONE...

"...THAT ONE WAS ON ME."

OKAY, SO LET ME SEE IF I'VE GOT THIS STRAIGHT.

APRIL.

LEONARDO.

RAPHAEL.

DONATELLO.

...AND CARAVAGGIO?

DUDE, IT'S *MICHELANGELO.* AS IN THE STATUE OF DAVID. HELLO? THE RESEMBLANCE IS UNCANNY.

WHAT ELSE CAN YOU TELL ME ABOUT THESE PORTALS? I'VE NEVER SEEN ANYTHING LIKE THEM.

WELL, WE HAVE. TOO MANY TIMES. THEY'RE BUILT AND CONTROLLED BY A GROUP OF ALIENS CALLED THE KRAANG.

WE THOUGHT THAT WE'D TAKEN THEM DOWN, BUT UNTIL TODAY, WE THOUGHT THE SAME THING ABOUT SNAKEWEED.

SENSEI?

I WAS LISTENING TO MY RADIO STATION, WHEN IT WAS INTERRUPTED.

CLICK

MASTER SPLINTER.

Ninjutsu expert. Kind-hearted father and sensei. Fan of 1980s smooth jazz.

...NO WORD ON THE EXACT THREAT CAUSING THIS WIDESPREAD PANIC. EYEWITNESS REPORTS HAVE VARIED FROM TALK OF ALIENS TO GIGANTIC SPIDERS.

LIVE AT 6 NEWS

CARLOS CHIANG O'BRIEN GAMBE

IT SEEMS THERE IS SOME SORT OF RIOT IN THE EAST VILLAGE.

WE NEED TO GET ON THIS, FAST. THAT COULD BE THE KRAANG OR—

HOLD ON. I'VE JUST LOCATED ANOTHER PORTAL. IT'S OVER IN CHINATOWN.

IT'LL HAVE TO WAIT. WE CAN'T AFFORD TO WASTE EVEN A—

WE SPLIT UP. LEONARDO AND RAPHAEL ARE WITH ME. WE'LL HEAD TO THE VILLAGE.

DONATELLO, YOU AND THE OTHERS LOCATE THE PORTAL. NO ONE GETS IN OR OUT.

GOT IT, BAT-BOSS.

DO YOUR BEST TO STAY OUT OF SIGHT...

20

"...WE DON'T WANT TO ATTRACT ANY MORE ATTENTION."

ANYBODY KNOW WHAT TIME IT IS?

IT'S TEN-THIRTY—

THAT'S RIGHT. IT'S MIKEY MIX TAPE TIME.

♪ WINGNUT, WINGNUT, RAP! ♪

WHAT ARE YOU DOING?

A SWEET HEAD BOP.

♪ WINGNUT, WINGNUT, RAP! ♪

COULD YOU PLEASE STOP?

I DON'T THINK THAT'S POSSIBLE.

♪ GO GO GO! ♪

WELL. THIS IS GONNA' BE A REAL HOOT.

♪ GO WINGNUT, GO WINGNUT, GO! ♪

CREATORS

MATTHEW K. MANNING

THE AUTHOR OF THE AMAZON BEST-SELLING *BATMAN: A VISUAL HISTORY*, MATTHEW K. MANNING HAS CONTRIBUTED TO MANY COMIC BOOKS, INCLUDING *BEWARE THE BATMAN*, *SPIDER-MAN UNLIMITED*, *PIRATES OF THE CARIBBEAN: SIX SEA SHANTIES*, *JUSTICE LEAGUE ADVENTURES*, *LOONEY TUNES* AND *SCOOBY-DOO, WHERE ARE YOU?* WHEN NOT WRITING COMICS, MANNING OFTEN WRITES BOOKS ABOUT COMICS, AS WELL AS A SERIES OF YOUNG READER BOOKS STARRING SUPERMAN, BATMAN AND THE FLASH. HE CURRENTLY LIVES IN NORTH CAROLINA, USA, WITH HIS WIFE, DOROTHY, AND THEIR TWO DAUGHTERS, LILLIAN AND GWENDOLYN.
VISIT HIM ONLINE AT WWW.MATTHEWKMANNING.COM.

JON SOMMARIVA

JON SOMMARIVA WAS BORN IN SYDNEY, AUSTRALIA. HE HAS BEEN DRAWING COMIC BOOKS SINCE 2002. HIS WORK CAN BE SEEN IN *GEMINI*, *REXODUS*, *TMNT ADVENTURES* AND *STAR WARS ADVENTURES*, AMONG OTHER COMICS. WHEN HE IS NOT DRAWING, HE ENJOYS WATCHING FILMS AND PLAYING WITH HIS SON, FELIX.

GLOSSARY

adapt change in order to survive

audience people who watch or listen to a play, film or show

bulb underground plant part from which some plants grow

criminal someone who has committed or is committing a crime

dorm room room shared by students living in university accommodation in the United States

dysfunctional different from what is considered normal

evolve when something develops over a long time with gradual changes

explosive chemical that can blow up

eyewitness someone who has seen something take place and can describe what happened

keenest having the greatest ability to notice things easily

neglect fail to do something

precision with accuracy

resemblance look similar to another person or thing

riot large group of people who use violence to show their anger or fear

sensei Japanese martial arts instructor

uncanny remarkable and difficult to explain

DISCUSSION QUESTIONS AND WRITING PROMPTS

1. DOES THE DETONATOR IN THE JOKER'S HAND REMIND YOU OF ANYTHING? WHY DO YOU THINK THE ARTIST CHOSE TO DRAW THE DEVICE THIS WAY?

2. HOW DOES SNAKEWEED ADAPT IN THE PANELS TO THE LEFT? WHAT ANIMALS IN REAL LIFE CAN YOU THINK OF THAT HAVE SIMILAR TYPES OF ADAPTATIONS?

3. BASED ON MICHELANGELO'S AND DONATELLO'S FACIAL EXPRESSIONS, HOW DO THEY FEEL ABOUT BATGIRL SINGING ALONG TO THE SONG?

4. WHAT CLUES ARE THERE IN THE PANELS BELOW THAT THE TURTLES' MINDS ARE BEING AFFECTED BY FEAR GAS?

READ THEM ALL!

BATMAN TEENAGE MUTANT NINJA TURTLES
ADVENTURES